This Storybook Belongs to:
Princess ________________________________

Sleeping Beauty

Jewels to Rule By

Princess Aurora awoke to the morning sun streaming into her room. She had just had the most wonderful dream! In it, she and Prince Phillip were married and living in a magnificent castle. Together, they ruled a beautiful kingdom filled with happy and loyal subjects.

"Someday," the Princess thought sleepily.

After Aurora had gotten up and dressed, her mother came in to greet her. "Good morning, sleepyhead!" said the Queen. "Finish getting ready and come along with me, my dear. I have something important to show you."

"What is it, Mother?" Aurora asked.

"Just follow me," the Queen answered, "You'll see soon enough."

The Queen led the Princess down a long hallway lined with portraits. Each one depicted a young woman wearing the same bejeweled crown. The Queen stopped before a painting of herself. "This is what I wanted to show you," she said.

"It's a lovely painting, Mother," Aurora said, "but I don't understand. I've seen this picture many times before."

"You are now at the age I was when that portrait was painted," the Queen explained. "The age at which I inherited the crown I now wear—and the age at which my mother and every queen back through the generations of my family inherited it. Now the time has come for the crown to be passed down to you."

"Oh, Mother!" exclaimed Aurora. "It's beautiful! I shall treasure it always!"

"I know you will," the Queen replied. "But before it is yours, there is an important task you must complete."

"What is that?" asked Aurora.

"The centerpiece of the crown is its three precious jewels," her mother replied. "It is up to you to determine what each gem symbolizes to you. In this way, you will discover the main principles that will guide you as a ruler."

"Oh, my," replied Aurora, a bit overwhelmed. "I don't even know where to begin."

The Queen smiled. "Never fear. You will have help from those who know you best. Good luck, and remember: If you listen to your heart, you will find the answers you seek."

The Princess was overjoyed to see that her three beloved fairy friends—Flora, Fauna, and Merryweather—had come to lend a hand.

"Rose! We've missed you!" exclaimed Merryweather. "We want to know everything that's happened since you came back to live at the castle . . . and don't leave anything out!"

"Merryweather," Flora said, "there's plenty of time for catching up later. Besides, the most important thing is that our Rose is happy—it's as plain as the nose on your face! Now, let's get down to business!"

"Thank you, darlings," said the Princess. "Because I'm afraid I don't even know where to begin!"

"Well, let's start with the diamond that's my favorite color," said Flora. "Pink! What does the color pink make you think of?"

"Hmmm," said Aurora as they strolled through the garden. "Oh! Roses, of course. And how when I lived with you in the forest, you called me 'Briar Rose.'"

"Did you learn anything as Briar Rose that might help you when you become Queen one day?" prodded Fauna.

The Princess was quiet for a moment. "Well, I know what it's like to be an ordinary member of the kingdom," she said, "so when I rule, I won't forget to take care of those who need my help most."

"Splendid, child!" replied Flora.

"Now let's think about the white diamonds in the crown," Fauna suggested. "What does the first one symbolize?"

Aurora sat down beside a fountain to ponder Fauna's question.

"Look down at your reflection in the water," Merryweather suggested. "See how the sun makes it sparkle all over?"

"Shush!" scolded Flora, "Aurora needs to decide what it means on her own!"

"I know!" said Aurora. "A diamond reflects light! A ruler should always be a beacon of light to her people, and bring them hope in times of darkness."

"Exactly!" replied Merryweather, giving Flora a satisfied smile.

"I've missed you all so much," Aurora said suddenly, giving each fairy a kiss. "Thank you so much for helping me today."

"It is an honor, my dear," Merryweather replied. "Now come, you're almost done! There's just one more diamond left to make sense of."

Aurora was delighted to discover Prince Phillip waiting for them at the stables.

"What a lovely surprise!" declared the Princess. "Have you come for a visit?"

"The Prince has come to help you uncover the meaning of the last diamond," explained Flora. "Now, gaze into the Prince's eyes and tell us what you feel."

"Love," Aurora said without hesitation. "Now let me see . . . love lasts forever—just like a diamond. A good ruler should always love her kingdom and all those who dwell within it!"

"You did it!" the fairies announced. "The Queen is going to be so pleased!"

They all headed straight back into the castle, where Aurora told her mother what each diamond in the crown represented.

The Queen smiled broadly. "Aurora, you are more than ready to inherit the crown which has been worn by each generation before you."

While Prince Phillip and the three fairies looked on, the Queen removed her crown and placed it on Aurora's head

"Now there is just one more tradition to be carried out to make the passing of the crown complete," the Queen said.

She summoned the royal painter, who set about creating a beautiful portrait of the Princess to hang in the grand hall alongside those of her ancestors.

That night, a grand ball was held to celebrate the Princess's inheritance of the crown.

"Wear it well," the Queen told Aurora. "Your intelligence and caring heart will make you a wonderful ruler indeed."

"Well, our work here is done," said Flora. "Time to fly!"

Merryweather hesitated. She was just itching to go back and change Princess Aurora's gown—and the pink diamond in her crown—to blue!